SHADOWS BENEATH THE FALLING SNOW

AN ELVEN KING PREQUEL STORY

CRISTINA RAYNE

For all lovers of elven stories

The Vampire Underground

Tales from the Vampire Underground: A Prequel Anthology

A Whisper in the Darkness *coming Spring 2018

Incarnations of Myth

Seeking the Oni *coming Jan 2018

Fractured Multiverse

(Writing as C.G. Garcia)

The Supreme Moment: Kairos

The Supreme Moment: Externus *coming Summer 2018

Black Crimson *coming Fall 2018

The Golden Mage

(Writing as C.G. Garcia)

The Kingdom of Eternal Sorrow

The Man Within the Temple

The Last Stone Cast

CHAPTER 1

When Miriel saw King Kirion for the first time, her first thought was, *Mother was wrong.*

Her mother had once described the supreme ruler of the Second Realm as a being who was cold, powerful, but exuded an almost terrible beauty as his presence alone tended to both awe and overwhelm all those who dared get close. Now, as she stood beside her mother, Queen Isilya's throne seat, Miriel couldn't help but stare as the king approached the dais. Hair, the color of pure gold, flowed over his shoulders to mid-waist like golden threads of silk. The contrast of that brilliant color was quite striking against the dark blue of his robes. No, there was nothing "cold" about this man. Rather, his very presence seemed on fire.

Keeping a neutral expression, she watched King

Kirion nod his head in acknowledgment to the two Lithviri monarchs. Then her parents rose and stepped down from the dais to welcome the king with a deeper bow of their heads.

"The Royal House of Nalldir and the Lithviri welcome Your Majesty to our lands," her father, King Arandur, said.

Not for the first time, Miriel wondered why King Kirion had decided to visit *now* of all times. Never mind that the last time he had come to their city had been before she was born, but to come on the winter solstice...well, it was unheard of for the reigning monarch to leave the performance of his kingdom's own sacred ceremonies to another.

Her father waved a hand behind him, beckoning her brother, Elion, and her forward. Miriel stepped beside her mother again and bowed deeply to their visitor, careful to keep her eyes down. Out of the corner of her eye, she could see Elion do the same. That was the first time she had ever seen her brother bow to anyone except their father, driving home the importance of the Sidhe standing before them.

"It has been far too long," King Kirion commented as he took in the entirety of her family with a single sweep of his eyes, his deep voice reverberating with a power that she could physically feel down to her very bones.

Miriel surreptitiously peeked at the king as she straightened. She could literally feel the aura of his proximity as well as the intensity of his gaze even though his eyes remained fixed on her father as they continued to exchange pleasantries. It was as though the surrounding air had thickened exponentially and had begun squeezing her tightly. It made her want to both flee and prostrate herself completely at his feet.

She settled for standing rigidly and averting her eyes to the rest of the court. Her mother's words had not quite captured the true essence of this experience. His presence alone had her quaking in her shoes. What would it be like to have those eyes filled with the knowledge of thousands of years look directly at her?

Miriel was once again uncomfortably reminded about a conversation she'd had with her father the previous day when he had informed her that King Kirion was to be present during their winter solstice festivities this year.

"Our supreme ruler has not set foot in these lands in perhaps two hundred years. Given the timing, I cannot think that it is merely for an exchange of pleasantries. You and Elion must both be diligent."

At the time, his words had filled her with a sense of unease. She had never been very good at navigating the various intrigues of the elven court, especially given the

—secretive nature of her past history, a history that none but three others knew existed. As a result, it was rare to see her at any social engagement far from Queen Isilya's side, her mother acting as her shield from all potentially dangerous questions. Thus, she had earned herself a reputation for being shy, something she had no plans of discouraging at all.

Miriel had thought her father had meant she would have to be doubly careful of King Kirion learning her secret, but now as she listened to the amiable tones of the two monarchs, she couldn't help but wonder if her father had been hinting at something else entirely. She had passed her hundredth year over a decade ago. She was already long past the time when a princess of the House of Nalldir was expected to marry…

Her eyes flickered over to King Kirion for another quick peek once Elion's voice entered the conversation. Her brother was perhaps as rigid as she as he bore the full brunt of the king's attention while they conversed in low, serious tones.

Miriel relaxed minutely. Surely his business concerned the Realm as a whole and not anything as commonplace as seeking a new wife. There had been no death announcement of his queen, and even if she *was* deceased, the Royal House of Elerren *always* married one from the Orviri House of Vanvir as per that ancient agreement between the two Sidhe races. The Lithviri had never minded ceding the supreme queen's throne to the Orvir Sidhe, and she saw no reason why her father would wish to change that now, much less make any kind of arrangement without at least talking to her about it first.

She was abruptly jolted out of her thoughts by a soft brush against her hand, and her eyes immediately turned to her mother. For a brief moment, Miriel saw a hint of worry in the queen's eyes before she was ushered back to fall into a single line facing the court with her father and brother while King Kirion stood in the forefront in order to receive any nobles who wished to greet the supreme ruler personally. She sighed inwardly. She *really* hated these court sessions involving visiting dignitaries. They always seemed to go on for days instead of a few marks. With someone as important as King Kirion, she feared the greetings would literally go on well into the night.

At least I have tomorrow evening to look forward to, she tried to comfort herself as she watched with growing dismay every single noble in attendance begin to queue up for a chance to speak with the supreme king.

However, within half a mark of passively watching her people welcoming the king with very little variation, her mother once again discreetly brushed her hand.

"Your father and Elion will represent our family for the remaining duration," Queen Isilya whispered. "We must attend to the rest of our duties. Come."

Miriel didn't need to be told twice. The two royals quietly left the throne room through the king's entrance behind the dais. Everyone was so fixated on King Kirion that she doubted their absence would even be noticed.

"He only looked at you once in greeting," her mother said as soon as they were out of earshot of the guards protecting the door they had just exited. "I feared his reason for coming was to ask for your hand, but now it appears I was mistaken."

"But his queen still lives, does she not?" Miriel asked, still anxious despite her mother's reassuring words.

"Yes. However, it has been nearly six thousand years since their union, and the throne of the Second Realm remains without a direct heir. It is not unheard of for the supreme ruler to take on a second wife if the first fails to produce a viable heir. That is not a life I would ever wish for you, but should His Supreme Majesty ask, your father would have no reason to refuse without it being seen as a great insult to the House of Elerren."

"I can think of one reason," Miriel said softly as they began to ascend the stairs to the royal wing.

"It has been well over a hundred years now," her

mother said firmly, "and I have not heard so much as a whisper of suspicion."

"But you said so, yourself. King Kirion is *different*— powerful. Standing so near to him today, I could literally feel that power. You are still worried." Miriel smiled wryly. "I can see your worry in your eyes no matter how you try to hide it."

The queen shook her head. "That worry is for *all* of us. If not to seek a new bride, what other dire situation would have him leave his lands without its king on such an important day as the solstice?"

"I wondered that myself," Miriel admitted.

"For now, all we can do is prepare ourselves for tomorrow's various ceremonies. We shall know if our worries are warranted soon enough."

CHAPTER 2

Miriel couldn't help scrutinizing both the faces of her father and King Kirion as both monarchs conversed in low tones at the high table while the rest of the nobles celebrated the solstice with music and dancing within the palace's great hall. As always, she sat next to her mother, politely refusing any offers to dance with her usual shy smile. After all this time, she wondered why anyone still bothered with her at all, especially when everyone believed her reticence was because her father had promised her to the heir to the Malviri throne.

Neither king looked anything other than calm, their bodies relaxed. Even the power King Kirion had been radiating since he had first appeared in the throne room was noticeably muted. Really, their appearance was of two old friends catching up after a long absence. Still,

Miriel couldn't relax, not quite able to shake the feeling that their calm was merely the calm before the storm. They had, after all, along with Elion, spent the entire evening and most of the night talking about the High Powers-only-knew what. Even her mother did not know what had been said as she had not gotten the chance to speak privately with her husband before the various rituals of the winter solstice had begun.

Not wanting to get caught staring, Miriel turned her eyes back to the dancers. Her eyes immediately picked out Elion and his wife as they gracefully twirled among the couples. Her expression turned wistful. What she wouldn't give to be able to join them. If only she dared to allow someone to touch her, to feel the embrace of someone other than her family...

She mentally shook herself. There was no use in wishing for something that quite possibly could never be. No matter how much her mother insisted that enough time had passed without incident, Miriel knew that she would never stop worrying that someone would learn her secret.

A few of the unwed, noble daughters hovered in small groups of three and four near the high table. Rumors of their supreme king's purpose in their lands had been running rampant throughout the palace since before the king's arrival yesterday, and the consensus seemed to be, as Miriel and her mother initially had believed, that King Kirion sought a second bride. Given that everyone already believed her promised to another, perhaps they hoped to catch the eye of King Kirion, especially now in this more casual setting where he was infinitely more approachable. Her mother may not wish for *her* to become a Royal Consort, even to the supreme king, but the fact remained that it was a very coveted and prestigious position.

Miriel wholeheartedly wished them success. As long as she remained within eyesight of King Kirion, there was no way the queen would allow her to excuse herself from the hall for the night as was her usual habit during these types of celebrations, but especially during the winter solstice. More than the bonding rituals with the land that her father performed every year that were important for every Sidhe under his rule, this day held even more meaning to Miriel in the form of a secret that not even her parents knew. It was one she feared they would forbid her from indulging in should they ever learn it. Having the young nobles dance with the king would provide the distraction she needed to slip out unnoticed.

However, after another mark had come and gone, it was beginning to seem as though King Kirion had no desire to indulge the hopefuls, and it was becoming increasingly harder for Miriel to hide her impatience. She chanced another look at him and was startled to meet the gaze of the king as he looked back at her with a rather impassive expression. Just how long had he been looking at her? She smiled politely and gave him a nod of acknowledgment before turning her attention to her mother without waiting to see what reaction, if any, he would give her.

"I guess His Highness does not wish to indulge in the dance this evening," Miriel remarked softly, hoping her mother would offer further information.

The queen looked back at her thoughtfully. "He is not known to indulge in such things, no, but I have only been to the supreme king's palace three times in my life and never during such an important celebration as the solstice. However—I am certain he would accept if I were to offer your hand for a dance." The last was said with a hint of a question.

Miriel smiled tightly. "You know why that cannot be, Mother. Besides, I was merely making an observation. It just seems a shame that you are also missing out in an activity you love while you both play host. Although *I* cannot offer to partner him, there are plenty of others to offer in my stead."

Her mother started to answer but broke off mid-word when both kings suddenly rose and began making their way towards them. Miriel felt herself go rigid as she watched them approach. It was all she could do to struggle to keep her growing anxiety from her expression as she stiffly followed her mother to her feet to receive them.

"My pardon, my ladies," King Kirion said, his voice still seemingly cutting straight through her, "but I must withdraw from the festivities for a moment." Then suddenly the full weight of his gaze was leveled at her. "I would hope you both would join our conversation when I return."

"It would be my pleasure, Your Majesty," Miriel found herself saying politely, not entirely sure what to make of his words, fairly innocuous words, had they been said by any other. If only she could get a read from her father, but his expression gave nothing away.

Nodding to the queen, King Kirion left the great hall, three of his guards trailing him. Miriel studied his back as he left, but his demeanor still did not betray what he was really thinking.

She turned to her father. "Is everything all right?"

A strange emotion flashed in his eyes, but it was gone before she could try to decipher it. "That remains to be seen," he replied enigmatically.

"Father…" Miriel trailed off, not sure what she wanted to ask or even if she should ask anything at all.

The king smiled and leaned over to kiss her on her forehead. "Do not worry, my little Elle. Whatever our supreme king's purpose here, it is not the one I initially feared."

Miriel frowned. That did little to alleviate her own anxiety as her father never did specify what those fears were.

He held out his arm to her. "Come. Let us join your brother in the dance while we await His Majesty's return."

CHAPTER 3

Sitting alone back at the high table, Miriel watched her parents closely as they danced among the courtiers, waiting for her best chance to fall out of their line-of-sight. The moment her parents' backs were turned to her, Miriel quickly slipped into the crowd and headed for the exit. At the door, one of the palace guards silently fell into step behind her.

"I am going up to the royal wing for a moment," she informed him over her shoulder.

True enough, but that didn't mean she planned on staying for long. She had no idea how long King Kirion would be away or how long he planned to socialize with them when he returned. This was probably her only chance to continue on with her usual solstice plans, if only for a few moments. It would have to be enough.

Once in her bedroom, Miriel spared only a few moments to grab her hooded cloak and to change her slippers to a pair of ankle-high boots more suited for walking through snow should she encounter it this year. Then she headed for the balcony.

The night air was chilly, but pleasantly so after the stifling warmth of the great hall. She walked over to the stone balustrade and leaned over slightly to peer into the darkness of her garden far below. Occasionally, the palace guards would patrol the pleasure gardens, and after nearly getting caught sneaking out of the palace by one such guard a couple of years ago, Miriel always made sure her garden was empty before descending.

When she was certain there was no one below, her eyes swept the balconies of both her parents' suite and that of the guest rooms as an extra precaution, but they were all empty. Satisfied, Miriel walked over to where the circular balustrade met the palace wall and reached out to tug on the thick vines growing along the wall, testing their strength until she was certain they would hold her weight.

With one final glance around to make certain that she was alone, Miriel carefully climbed onto the balustrade, her hands grabbing onto a couple of thick vines tightly before she reached out a leg to find a foothold within the tangled stems and leaves. Once secure, she slowly began her decent.

"That is certainly an interesting way of entering your garden," a deep voice suddenly remarked from somewhere above her, making Miriel almost lose her hold when she jumped nearly out of her skin.

Tightening her grip, she looked up wildly at her balcony, her heart threatening to tear out of her chest, but she could see no one. She was close to the bottom, so she opted to just jump down the rest of the way. Once on the ground, she began to frantically inspect all the balconies within sight above her, but they all appeared just as empty as before.

"Up here, on the perimeter wall," that same voice said with a hint of amusement.

Miriel froze. She finally recognized that voice. Of all the people to catch her now…

She slowly turned around and lifted her gaze upwards. And there King Kirion sat along the top of the wall, his legs dangling over the far edge and his upper body twisted around in order to stare down at her. He was too far up for her to see his face properly, and that fact made her heart begin to beat more frantically. What in the name of the High Powers was he doing up *there*?

"Your Majesty," she greeted with a bow of her head, not sure what else to do in this awkward situation.

"Out for a breath of this wonderful mountain air?" he asked without any discernable inflection.

A question full of many traps. *This* was why she had stuck so closely to her mother's side ever since the supreme king had arrived, fearing to be caught alone with this powerful elf. There was no way she had the skill to match wits with a mind that had lived for millennia.

However, she forced herself to look up at him again even though what she really wanted to do was run away. "Something like that," she agreed but did not elaborate. "It seems we had the same thought," she added, hoping to steer the conversation away from herself.

He regarded her silently for a long, uncomfortable moment. Miriel could feel the tension rising in her shoulders as she struggled not to fidget beneath his scrutiny. Although he was at least three stories above her, she could feel his gaze on her as though his eyes were physically touching her.

Then suddenly, between one blink and the next, the king disappeared.

What in the— was all her bewildered mind managed before King Kirion just as abruptly faded into view only a step before her, causing her to flinch away.

"Apologies," he said. "I did not mean to startle you. I just assumed you knew of my phasing ability."

Oh, of course. Miriel relaxed minutely.

She shook her head and offered him a small smile. "No apologies needed, Your Majesty. My mother did speak of it to me once, but the reality of it was —surprising."

"Would you care to join me up above? I would very much enjoy speaking with you for a moment before we must rejoin the celebrations."

Miriel's heart sank. Though the cold would likely drive them indoors within a mark or so, King Kirion would definitely insist on escorting her back to the great hall. Once back under the gaze of her parents, there was no way she would be given the opportunity to sneak out a second time.

Seeing no way around it, she simply nodded, afraid her voice would betray her disappointment.

It was only when he had already stepped closer and his arms were sliding around her waist that she realized with sudden panic that he was *touching* her. Then the world all around them blurred, and she was standing on top of the perimeter wall before she could even finish gasping. Miriel instinctually clutched at his robes as a cold gust of wind hit her, then immediately dropped her hands to her sides in horror. One did not simply grab onto the supreme king for any reason!

Seemingly unaware of her distress, King Kirion

released her and then stepped over to the edge where he proceeded to settle himself down in his previous position. Miriel stood frozen for a few tense beats before she forced her legs to move. She carefully seated herself beside him with about an arms-length of distance between them, making a big show of arranging her skirts in order to give herself time to calm down.

He had touched her, and by some miracle, it did not appear as though he had noticed anything amiss. She didn't want to press her luck by allowing him a second chance.

"Do you enjoy high places?" Miriel asked, once again trying to steer the conversation away from herself.

"Just places where I cannot be easily disturbed," he replied.

Miriel bowed her head. "Then I am sorry that I intruded on your solitude."

"You did not," he assured her. "I chose to call out to you, remember?"

She glanced back at him. His eyes were fixed on her in that same intense, unfathomable expression he had worn since the first time she had seen him. She quickly looked back down at the hands she had threaded in her lap.

"You must think me strange."

"More a curiosity rather than strange," he said. "I

simply did not expect to see the mild-mannered and shy Lithviri princess climbing down the face of the palace with such practiced skill—in her court finery no less. Were you perhaps off to meet someone you did not wish others to see?"

Miriel couldn't help the short laugh that burst from her lips at his bluntness. "I always feared that were I caught, that would be the king and queen's first thought as well, and that they would not believe any of my protests."

"Word has it that Arandur has promised you to the Malviri heir. As it is not a love match, I would not find it amiss that you had a paramour."

She looked at him sharply. "You have heard that rumor even in your own lands?"

His eyes narrowed slightly. "Rumor?"

She nodded, shifting a bit in sudden discomfort. This was *not* something she should even be discussing with the supreme king, but she only had herself to blame for encouraging his questions instead of trying to redirect their conversation to a safer, more appropriate subject.

"My father has made no such offer to the Malviri king," she admitted reluctantly. She paused and then added a bit sheepishly, "I have a habit of walking alone, away from the crowds and noise, for at least a couple of marks every solstice. It is a time for me, alone, to remember the past, a time that even my parents do not know I indulge in. The palace guards would insist on accompanying me were I to enter my garden the usual way. Thus, I use the vines instead."

"Understandable," he said as he turned his gaze outward to the mountains in the distance.

At that moment, the supreme king looked so sad. It made Miriel want to reach out and lay a hand onto his shoulder in comfort. She gripped her skirt tightly in both fists to prevent herself from acting so rashly.

"The past can be a heavy burden," he continued, his eyes still fixed on some point ahead. "That is why I am pleased to share this, my own time of solitude, with you on this night."

"I—am barely into my second century of life," she ventured hesitantly. "I cannot even fathom the weight of a millennium, much less eight. I am not certain how much comfort I can offer you, Your Majesty."

"Your presence, alone, is enough," he said. He turned to her, the heat of his gaze cutting straight into her so that her chest seized painfully in a surge of confusing emotions.

And then he smiled.

It was just a small upturn of the corners of his lips, but the effects on an already exquisite face were breathtaking. Even in the darkness, his face seemed to radiate with light, his eyes ignite with a spark of power, with *life*. It was singularly the most beautiful and terrifying thing she had ever witnessed, and it left her momentarily too stunned to even *think*, much less react.

That's why when Kirion reached for her hand, Miriel didn't even have the presence of mind to draw it away. The coolness of his hand around her own slightly warmer flesh jolted her from her fascination, and her eyes shot down to their joined hands in something akin to panic. He was touching her again!

It was done. There was nothing left but to raise her eyes and face the consequences of her carelessness. Through sheer will alone, she calmed her racing heart and looked up into his face.

CHAPTER 4

The king's expression was intense, but there was none of the expected anger, the accusation she had feared for the majority of her life. If anything, there was only a hint of puzzlement in his eyes for a brief moment before Miriel felt him squeeze her hand lightly. Could it be that her mother had been right all along? Had enough time passed that she no longer had to fear the discovery of her secret?

"Miriel?" he inquired, a thousand questions buried within his tone.

"I—forgive me, Your Majesty," she said, then decided that a little truth was needed here. "I am not accustomed to the touch of others and was momentarily startled." She tentatively squeezed his hand in what she hoped was reassurance.

His eyes grew thoughtful. "Arandur did mention that

you were a sensitive soul, though I did not think he had meant it so literally. My very presence must weigh heavily on you as the strength of my soul is considerable."

"I do not mind," was all she could think to say.

She was digging herself more deeply into the lies she was accustomed to telling, much more than she had ever intended with this powerful being. She should *not* have allowed King Kirion to continue believing her dislike of being touched was due to a strong empathic ability, but...

He turned his head back to stare out at the nightscape before them before he spoke again. "You must have questions," he said, "about why I have come to your lands."

"It is not for me to question," Miriel said diplomatically, though her heart sped up a little in anticipation. "As my father has not spoken of it to me, then he must not have felt it was something I needed to know. It is enough that Elion is aware."

"Or it is simply that he has not found the opportunity."

Miriel stiffened. What was he trying to say? Her thoughts flashed back to the conversation she'd had with her mother yesterday.

"I feared his reason for coming was to ask for

your hand…"

Her eyes fell to their still-joined hands, and she swallowed nervously, suddenly feeling extremely shy. "Perhaps…" she replied.

Kirion turned to look at her again, and Miriel nearly gasped at the strength of the melancholia in his eyes. It was the last thing she expected to see.

"The whole of the Second Realm is currently on the brink of a great change," he said. "Although the signs have been present for some time, few have seen them for what they are. In fact, those very signs are the reason why I have sought solitude on the night of the winter solstice for thousands of years. You are, of course, aware that the supreme throne has no direct heir?"

She blinked at him curiously. "Yes."

The king sighed, suddenly sounding weary. "What the Realm does not know, outside of a handful of souls, is that for the space of a mark several thousand years ago, the throne did indeed have an heir."

Miriel's eyes widened. But that would mean—why in the world was he telling *her* this momentous secret?

"You had a son," she said softly, a wave of sadness washing through her at the flash of pain in his eyes that he could not quite hide.

He nodded. "Almost from the first moment that I was able to sense my son's soul, the queen became deathly ill, so ill that her healer feared for not only the child's life but the mother's. Thus, the queen was kept in seclusion for the duration of the pregnancy, and the imminent birth was never revealed publicly in preparation for the worst. I need not tell you the stigma associated with such an ill-fated birth."

"No," she agreed.

"That I both gained and lost a son on the night of the winter solstice, on a day that celebrates our life-bond to our lands, it filled me with such terrible grief that it blinded me to the calamity our people will soon face until very recently."

"And you have spoken to my father about this?" she asked.

"About my late son? No."

Miriel was more than taken aback. "Then why—"

Kirion smiled again, and her words instantly trailed off as she became lost in his beauty for the second time that night.

"There are some things that you, alone, need to understand," he said, lifting her hand to his lips to brush a light kiss onto the back, his eyes watching her face closely.

"My father—no, my *mother*—would never allow me to serve as a Royal Consort, even to the supreme king," she said slowly, not quite able to believe that they were even having this conversation.

He released her hand and deliberately slid closer to her until their sides were almost touching. He then slowly raised his hands and gently cupped her cheeks. She sat frozen, unsure how she was supposed to react, or even how she *wanted* to react.

"I do not seek a Royal Consort," he said quietly. "I have come to your lands in search of my new queen."

Then he leaned forward and captured her lips in a firm kiss before she could even make sense of his words. Her first instinct was to gasp, opening her mouth to a slick tongue that began to sensually caress along her own before it could shy away. She shivered at this entirely new sensation and closed her eyes, surrendering herself to his tongue and lips and attempting to reciprocate as she had no personal experience.

Miriel could feel the power of the supreme king even in his kiss, his lips demanding though somehow tender, making her want to give him her everything even though she had spent so little time with him. Her entire body felt hot even with the chill in the air as she unconsciously fisted her own skirts in reaction.

She could feel his warm exhales on her lips as he drew away what felt like an eternity later, tickling the now swollen, sensitive flesh. She opened her eyes to see him staring at her with eyes darkened with several emotions she could not readily name. It was only then that her brain caught up to the present, and she realized the enormity of what had just happened. Although the supreme king had initiated the kiss with little warning, there was no denying that after she had gotten over her initial shock, she had enjoyed the kiss immensely.

"My—my king?" Miriel stuttered, confusion, desire, and shyness warring within her being.

Kirion rested his forehead against her own and closed his eyes. "Queen Althea has abdicated her throne," he said. "It was for the purpose of allowing another bride from the House of Vanvir to assume the title in the hope that she may give me the heir that Althea could not. However, they do not see what I see."

"What do you see?" Miriel breathed, her chest clenching painfully in reaction to a thousand unfamiliar emotions.

Kirion opened his eyes and pulled away to look at her solemnly. "That we are currently on the brink of another Plague of Infertility."

This time, Miriel did gasp aloud. The Plague of Infertility was something confined to the pages of their ancient history, something she had learned of but never thought would become a reality during her time.

"I thought—I thought the Sidhe of old conquered the affliction," she said uncertainly.

"As do most," he agreed. "However, only the symptom was addressed, and now the majority believes that what was only a temporary remedy was a cure. Already, there are a significantly lower amount of children being born throughout the Realm, especially within the Orvir Sidhe of my former queen. I fear infertility will strike the females of the House of Vanvir completely within the next generation, and the rest of the Houses will follow within the next thousand years. It is my greatest wish to leave any future children I may have with the best chances to prolong the future of my bloodline.

"The birthrate has not yet diminished as significantly here among the Lithviri. Thus I traveled here during this interim time in which a bride has not yet been chosen for me and will not be chosen until the summer solstice. My plan was to stay here among the Lithviri for the span of two seasons in order to find a suitable bride." He flashed her a wry smile. "I did not expect the Lithviri princess to peak my interest by climbing the vines so fearlessly tonight."

Miriel dropped her eyes, unsure how to react to his comment. "I cannot imagine how witnessing me behaving in such an undignified manner would interest one of your experience," she said softly.

"It is that very thing that interests me," he said earnestly, causing her to look up at his face again. He raised a hand and lightly ran his fingertips across her cheek in an affectionate caress that made her skin tingle. "At that moment, I was able to see a piece of your true essence free of the constraints of your rank. It draws me like few things have over these past few centuries."

"But—" she began, then realized she had no idea what she really wanted to say. Her mind was currently a maelstrom of confusing emotions thanks to his sudden, utterly unexpected kiss. She had no idea how she should feel about it, about everything he had just told her.

Kirion leaned over and kissed her on the forehead. "You need not answer me tonight," he said. "As I said, I did not expect to feel such a strong interest so soon after my arrival." He glanced over his shoulder. "Besides, it is probably long past time that we rejoin the festivities. We shall have plenty of time to speak, to spend time together, in the days to come if that is what you wish."

Miriel couldn't help the smile that stretched her lips. "It would be my pleasure," she said sincerely.

However confused and uncertain she was feeling about the kiss they had shared, the one thing she was certain of was that she wanted to talk with him more.

Whatever she had been expecting the supreme king to be, it was not this frank, entirely approachable person sitting next to her on the perimeter wall of all things. It was a far cry from the powerful being she had first glimpsed in the throne room that had her almost quaking in her shoes.

She wondered if he was, in fact, going out of his way to keep his power in check, if this gentler side of him was a façade or if she had actually glimpsed a bit of his true character. Well, only time would tell, and at the moment, she was more than willing to give him that. Now that another had touched her and proven her fears had been for naught, for the first time in her life, Miriel felt that the future was completely open to her at last.

"Shall I escort you back to your balcony?" Kirion asked with a hint of amusement.

Miriel hesitated. Midnight was probably still a couple of marks or so away. If she hurried, she still had time to continue on with at least some of her earlier plans. The question was whether or not she could persuade the king to leave her to it.

"If you do not mind, Your Majesty," she said, "can you take me down into the garden instead? There is still something I wish to do before returning to the great hall."

"Oh?" he asked with more interest than she would have liked.

She flashed him an apologetic smile. "Just as you have things you wish to remember in solitude on this night, I have a place I wish to visit in solitude as well. Rest assure that I shall be along before long."

Kirion studied her for a long, anxious moment before he finally nodded and said, "As you wish."

Once again, Miriel found herself wrapped in his arms and the world fading away. A breath later, she felt the ground beneath her feet.

"Thank you," she said, feeling his arms loosen from her body as she stepped away. It was not nearly as cold here on the ground, but she found herself shivering anyway, missing his warmth and a bit discomfited about that realization.

He nodded. "Perhaps you will honor me with a dance when you return."

Her eyes lit up. "I would enjoy that very much, Your Majesty."

Then with one final nod, the king faded from view, leaving her to ponder the complexity of the supreme king.

CHAPTER 5

Miriel quietly stepped through the gate that separated her garden from the queen's garden, her eyes darting all around her in the darkness in search of any possible guards, but the area was still. She could hear the faint sounds of laughter and music from deep within the palace, and for a moment, a surge of worry flowed through her.

By now, King Kirion had no doubt rejoined her parents at the high table, and they would be wondering where she had run off to. Unsure of whether or not the supreme king had revealed his intentions of finding a bride to her father, he would not necessarily inform them of their chance meeting, nor of her promise to return to the great hall as soon as her business was concluded.

Nevertheless—Miriel had been looking forward to

this night all year, and it was a relief that she still had enough time before the solstice ended to enjoy what she had come to consider her yearly treat.

She wrapped her cloak more tightly around her body as a gust of wind cut through her. It would probably snow again tonight. Although the elven mages prevented the snow from entering all the various gardens and the courtyard, the grounds beyond the wall would no doubt be full of the beautiful drifts that she loved. Perhaps she could even invite King Kirion for a walk among them.

The thought brought her up short. What in the world was she *thinking*? He was their supreme ruler! She had only spent less than a mark alone with him, and already he was beginning to permeate her thoughts as though she had known him all her life. How had her initial curiosity turned into *this* so quickly?

Now more than a little troubled, Miriel hurried through her mother's garden to the small copse of trees in the center, eager to take her mind off her encounter with the king for the moment. Fairly innocuous at first glance, this was the Royals' doorway into the Inbetween, the plane of existence between the elven and human realms.

With one final glance around to make certain that she was alone, Miriel stepped between a specific pair of trees and the dark of night was instantaneously replaced with the gray, hazy atmosphere ever-present within the Inbetween. Thick grass tickled her ankles as she hurried across the vast grassland, allowing her sense of the thickness of the air around her as always to guide her towards the secret spot she had stumbled upon twenty years ago.

Invisible to the naked eye, it had only been her curiosity of what was causing the strange heaviness in the air one night during the winter solstice that had led to this astonishing, wonderful discovery. She truly had been seeking solitude away from the laughing, dancing courtiers that only reminded her of the burden of the secret she carried. It was only when she had reached out a hand to touch the area where the air had seemed almost as substantial as water that she had found what she had come to call "The Rift."

Within moments, Miriel stood at the nexus of that heaviness. A surge of excitement flowed through her as she stepped forward, wondering what she would find this time. Then without warning, a hand grabbed one of her arms, jolting her to a halt halfway through The Rift as she cried out in shock. She whirled around, her heart in her throat—only to feel that same heart drop to the pit of her stomach when her eyes met the form of the supreme king.

She stood frozen, unable to form a single coherent thought as she stared up at King Kirion with wide eyes. She had been so focused on following the variances in the density of the air that she had failed to notice that she was being followed.

However, rather than a chastising look, his gaze only reflected a mild curiosity. "I suppose that 'place' you mentioned earlier is within the human realm," he said, nodding towards her body, which was already partially within The Rift and thus hidden from sight.

"You—followed me?" As soon as the words left her lips, Miriel winced internally. She hadn't meant for her question to sound so accusative.

His eyes bored down into her own. "Imagine my concern when your life-force abruptly vanished."

You can sense that? she wanted to ask, but instead forced herself to nod and relax her shoulders. "My apologies for causing you such concern, Your Majesty."

"Miriel," he said, raising his other hand to cup her cheek. "We are not among the elven court. There is no need for you to be so formal with me when we are alone."

She flashed him a sheepish smile, trying to ignore how soft and pleasantly warm the king's hand felt pressed against her cheek. "I still occasionally find myself speaking formally to my father when we are alone, the habit is so ingrained, but I shall try."

His gaze turned towards The Rift, and he frowned. "You have opened a curious type of pathway. I have never seen it done in this manner."

Miriel shrugged nervously. "I did not create it," she admitted but did not elaborate.

"Arandur, then," Kirion said thoughtfully, and Miriel didn't correct him, hoping that he would drop the subject altogether. He turned that thoughtful gaze back to her. "Is it truly a *place* that you wish to visit within the human realm?" he demanded suddenly.

"It is," Miriel said slowly, wondering at the strange undercurrents of emotion that she heard in his tone.

She paused and then turned to look at The Rift, but she couldn't yet see what lay beyond. Did she dare reveal this particular secret to him, one that not even her mother knew?

"Would you—would you like to accompany me?" Miriel asked hesitantly, looking back in order to gauge his expression. "It is better for you to see for yourself as I could never hope to describe it as it deserves."

Kirion released her arm and grasped her hand instead, threading their fingers together. "I have not had a more intriguing invitation in millennia," he said with a small smile. "Can you at least tell me which region we shall be visiting?"

Miriel smiled. "I believe I shall leave that as a surprise," she replied teasingly, marveling at her own audacity. Yesterday she would have sooner cut her own arm off rather than speak so freely and familiarly with the supreme king.

Then she pulled him through The Rift before he could comment. Her eyes were almost immediately assaulted by hundreds of colored lights, and Miriel couldn't help but let out a laugh in absolute delight. She had hoped that it would be this particular scene that would greet them. She turned to her companion excit-edly, but instead of wonder, Kirion's expression was alarmingly stone-faced and unreadable.

"Miriel...this is..." His tone was laced with some-thing akin to shock had it been anyone else speaking as his eyes slowly took in the forest of multi-colored lights before them.

And it *was* a forest—or at least a sizeable grove. They were currently standing at the entrance to a spectacle she had walked through over a dozen times over the past twenty years.

Miriel's chest clenched painfully in the beginnings of panic. His reaction was far from what she had expected. Had she just made a huge mistake in bringing him here?

It was almost as though seeing something that he obviously didn't understand had changed his entire demeanor to that of someone who had just witnessed an utterly unexpected danger.

She squeezed his hand uncertainly. "It's all right. There is no danger here."

"This is *not* the human realm," Kirion stated, his eyes remaining fixed on what was, for him, a scene that was totally alien.

"It is," she insisted. "Just—not the one anyone has ever seen. At least not yet."

"Not yet?" he echoed, looking down at her with a frown.

Miriel shook her head. "I am explaining this all wrong." She gestured behind them. "That doorway was not made by my father or, I suspect, anyone else."

Understanding flashed in his eyes. "A natural tear in the fabric of reality, then," he hazarded.

"That is what I believe, as well. I stumbled upon it twenty years ago. It is a doorway that only appears on the day of the winter solstice. At first, I was as confused by all of this as you are now, but after exploring the wonders of this place, I came to understand over the years that this is indeed the human realm—only a human realm far, far into the future."

Kirion's eyes narrowed sharply before he turned, his

hand tightening around her own as though fearful she would run off, and walked up to one of the nearest trees that lined the edges of a pathway just large enough for a carriage to navigate. Its limbs and trunk were wrapped with strings of seemingly hundreds of tiny lights of red, green, blue, and white. Their boots barely disturbed the snow-covered ground, a consequence of a Sidhe's inability to manifest completely within the human realm, one she had often lamented in the past.

He reached out his free hand and cautiously touched one of the blue lights. When it did not burn him, he grasped it between his thumb and index finger and lightly squeezed, his eyes scrutinizing.

"It is glass," he said finally after a long moment of silence broken only by the soft whistling of the wind. "However, even with my hand only half-manifested within this realm, I expected to feel at least a tinge of heat as this oddity burns within with energy." He released the light and turned to look at her rather intensely. "You have seen humans here in this place? It was they who illuminated the trees in this strange manner?"

Miriel nodded and then pointed to the north. "There is also a human town nearby, less than a mark away by foot. You need only visit it to see that their progress is eons beyond all the human settlements I have ever witnessed while entering into the human realm through the usual doorways. This spectacle before us was done in celebration of their own version of the solstice. They have lined many of their structures with these lights as well. The humans call it 'Christmas.'"

"I do not sense anything other than the local wildlife."

"It is probably well before dawn here. Each time I have stepped through The Rift, it is never the same day, never the same point of time during the day. There were times when I stepped out into the full light of midday. While The Rift within the Inbetween only opens during the winter solstice, what lies beyond is always a surprise. The only consistency has been that it is always within a few days of the solstice on this side."

"Why is it that you have not told your parents about such an extraordinary discovery?"

"I feared they would forbid me from returning, and my yearly visits to this place have become dear to me."

Kirion sighed. "They would be right to forbid you. The pathways opened naturally between the two realms are always unstable, dangerously so. Each time you step through is a time you risk becoming trapped here." He turned his gaze back to the beautifully illuminated trees, and his expression softened. "However, I can under-stand what draws you to return."

Miriel squeezed his hand excitedly. "Then allow me to show you more. This is merely the beginning of a path that leads to several displays of the humans' creations. I have witnessed many humans over the years either walking or riding a wagon along this same path and delighting in this visual spectacle as much as I."

As they walked, a light snow began to fall. It wasn't long before the tiny flakes morphed into a thick flurry. She imagined that if any of the humans could see them now, they would only appear to the human eye as shadows walking hand-in-hand beneath the falling snow. She couldn't decide if that would make for a romantic or unnerving sight.

A few flakes tickled her nose, and Miriel couldn't help but laugh in delight. "I love the way the snowflakes feel fluttering against my skin here in the human realm," she confessed at Kirion's questioning look, "no more substantial than a cool breath."

The king's lips quirked up slightly. "Not only snow, but I can very much see you delighting in a sudden downpour."

"I have been known to do that a time or two," she agreed with a smile. A slight curving of the path caught her eye, and her smile widened. "Oh! We are here!"

Momentarily forgetting that it was the *supreme king* she had by the hand, Miriel eagerly tugged Kirion forward around the last corner, and the illuminated trees gave way to a sizeable clearing full of the illuminated creations she wanted him to see. She then paused and turned her gaze back to her companion, excited to see his reaction.

Perhaps it was the result of thousands of years of habitually schooling his emotions, but the only reaction he showed was a slight widening of his eyes as he took in the scene before him. Various scenarios had been brought to life through the art of wires and multitudes of those tiny, multicolored lights. A few steps ahead, wire frames wrapped in strings of white lights in the unmistakable shapes of several deer were in the process of bending down as if to graze on the plant life peeking through the snow at their "hooves." A few steps from the deer, a cluster of mini trees created entirely by wire and lights seemed to twinkle similarly to the stars across the night sky.

Kirion released her hand and cautiously stepped towards one of the deer and silently watched as its head slowly dipped to the ground and rose back up over and over.

"How is this accomplished?" he asked as Miriel stepped up beside him.

"I am—not certain," she replied. "I have never seen them erected, only occasionally moved."

The king nodded and then his gaze fixed onto something beyond the wire trees. Miriel turned her attention from him—and nearly burst out laughing when she realized the object that had caught his attention.

"That is a representation of a figure the humans call 'Santa Claus,'" she offered, unable to completely keep the amusement from her voice. "Apparently, he brings gifts to all the human children every year during their Christmas celebration."

Kirion turned to her, his expression now clearly perplexed. "That does not seem possible."

Miriel shrugged. "Perhaps it is just a story."

"Perhaps."

They spent the next few moments just walking around and taking in all the various colorful creations. Occasionally, the king would ask her a question, but otherwise, he observed everything in silence. Miriel didn't mind. It was more than enough to be able to show him all of this. In fact, she was especially pleased that he was the first from the elven realm, other than her, to see this. When he had voiced a desire earlier to spend more time with her, he had probably never imagined that they would spend it marveling at these human creations.

"Here the final proof lies before me," Kirion suddenly said as they stood before a row of red and white hooked sticks, looking at her with eyes that seemed to pierce down to her very soul.

"Proof?" she repeated in confusion as she instinctually squirmed beneath his gaze.

He slowly cupped her face between his hands and rubbed his thumbs gently over her cheeks. "That you were once human."

CHAPTER 6

To have her deepest secret presented to her so bluntly was so shocking that all Miriel could do was freeze, her mind stuttering to a stop in a mixture of panic and fear, but not only that, she was stricken.

He will no longer want me.

Walking together among the light displays, feeling such joy at being able to share one of her few treasured activities with King Kirion made her realize just how much she had allowed him into her heart tonight. A human was no kind of partner for the supreme elven king, no matter how much she now looked like an elf.

"Please do not be angry, Your Majesty," Miriel begged. "My father only wished to protect me from censure. I know should have told you especially, but—"

Kirion abruptly leaned down and silenced her with his lips. Miriel was so shocked that she remained still and unresponsive, her mind unable to comprehend what was happening. He drew away after only a few soft caresses of his lips, but he continued to cradle her face between his hands.

"I am not angry, Miriel," he said quietly. "I knew from the moment that you and Elion stood before me yesterday in the throne room that you had a human soul."

"You...knew..."

He nodded. "It is not widely known, but I can easily read the souls of others as though they were the souls of my own children."

"Then why..." Miriel trailed off and lowered her eyes, unable to go on.

The king lifted her chin and commanded firmly, "Look at me."

She reluctantly complied. The weight of those ancient eyes as they gazed upon her was almost too much to bear, but she forced herself not to look away.

"You think yourself unworthy of me?" he guessed. When she remained silent, he released her chin and gathered her into his arms. "Did I not already confess how much the essence of your spirit has drawn me to you? I thought of little else but you from the moment we parted in your garden. Knowing that you were once human only strengthened my desire to know you, to experience the world through the eyes of someone who was more than Sidhe."

He sighed and hugged her more tightly against his body. Surprise and uncertainty kept her arms hanging loosely at her sides. "For one who has lived as long as me, your uniqueness is something I desire almost as desperately as my desire for a child, else I fear I may soon stagnate. No one else could be a worthier partner."

"You should not think so highly of my potential," Miriel whispered against his chest. "I shall only disappoint you."

"That you truly believe so is the very reason why you will not."

The king's tone held a strange note, and Miriel lifted her head to look up at him questionably. The intense look in his eyes as Kirion stared down at her made her shiver in both apprehension and something like excitement. No one had ever looked at her with such intensity.

"It has been perhaps centuries since I truly desired anything or anyone," he said. "I wish to show you just how much, here beneath the falling snow surrounded by this visual wonder, if you will allow me."

Slowly, Miriel raised her arms to encircle his waist,

returning his embrace as her mind whirled. To give herself so intimately to another—it was something she thought she would never experience, afraid that a touch alone would reveal her humanity. Although she had always been curious about the act, itself, she was almost shocked at how much she did want it, wanted to experience it with *him*. It seemed fitting that her first erotic experience could be here, a place where they both physically existed equally within the two realms.

"Yes," Miriel replied simply, and his answering smile was just as beautiful and mesmerizing as before.

Kirion released his hold on her waist and raised his hands to unclasp the broach at her neck in order to open her cloak. He slid the cloak from her shoulders and spread it out onto the snow-covered ground between the row of flashing candy canes and a large snowman that was illuminated brightly from within each of the three segments that composed its body. Then Miriel was suddenly lifted and tumbled onto the cloak, his lips hungrily seeking out her own before she could do more than gasp.

There was no reservation in the supreme king's kiss, his tongue plunging into her mouth even as he swallowed her gasp. This time, her tongue moved to slowly tangle with his, if a little tentatively. The new sensations made her shiver, and she gripped his shoulders tightly as he loomed over her, desperate for something to hold on to as she began to drown in so many new sensations and unfamiliar emotions.

One of the king's knees pressed between her oddly splayed legs, coaxing her to open them wider before he pushed the skirt of her dress up and moved in to settle his body between her thighs with a firm, aggressive thrust of his hips against her now-naked groin. She could feel his warmth even through his formal robes, and a sense of both nervous excitement and contentment washed through her.

It did not matter to her that they were virtually exposed here among the Christmas displays to anyone who happened to walk by, two shadows moving in the throws of passion. At that moment, the world only consisted of the tickling snowflakes falling down upon them and Kirion.

His lips moved down her chin to the base of her neck as his hands busied themselves with unlacing her bodice. She let out a surprised moan as Kirion's mouth fastened onto her pulse point and sucked hard. She found one of her hands lifting of its own accord from his shoulder to run through the golden hair that spilled over his shoulders and tickled her face, the delicate strands gliding over her fingers more softly than silk.

Miriel soon felt the cool air against her breasts as

they were finally freed from behind that thick, restrictive material. Kirion slid the palm of his hand teasingly along the curve of her left breast until he was cupping it in a firm, possessive grip, his fingers kneading. He moved his mouth down to the other, latching onto her nipple and proceeding to torment the rapidly hardening nub with both teeth and tongue as she writhed and gasped beneath him.

The king was moving so fast and aggressively that Miriel couldn't think straight. This close, the strength of his aura was also nearly overwhelming, enveloping her entire body until it felt as though she was being embraced by two men.

"Kirion," she half moaned, half pleaded, her fingers tightening their grip on both his shoulder and within his hair.

He raised his head, his eyes half-lidded with unmistakable lust that quickly melted into concern in reaction to something he must have seen in her expression. He cupped her cheek gently. "Did I hurt you?" he asked.

Miriel offered him a small smile and shook her head. "The power that naturally flows from your body can be somewhat overwhelming at times," she admitted.

Kirion surged up to kiss her lips softly. Already she could feel the pressure surrounding her lessen significantly.

"Better?" he asked, his mouth barely a breath away from her own.

Her lips brushed over his briefly when she nodded, making her tremble as a burst of sensation flooded the hypersensitive tissue. Then his mouth was pressing against hers firmly again, and her mind promptly became hazy with pleasure as he slowly began to grind his still-clothed hips against her naked groin. Miriel's arms wrapped around his neck and her thighs instinctually tightened around his hips as the soft material of his breeches rubbed deliciously against the center of her pleasure until she was wet and lifting her hips up in abandon to join him in his sensuous dance.

All too soon, Kirion stilled his hips, causing an involuntary noise of protest to burst from her lips. Miriel might have been embarrassed at her total loss of control had her mind not long been reduced to mush.

Kirion snaked a hand down between their bodies to where she throbbed between her legs, his fingers ghosting over her clit, making her instantly arch up against his hand in pursuit of more of that delicious friction.

Miriel tore her mouth away from his with a gasp. "Please—Kirion—I need…!" she begged, squeezing his neck desperately.

Kirion's lips quirked up slightly, and then he abruptly

thrust two of his fingers deeply into her passage. Miriel threw her head back with a cry at this new sensation. She clenched her inner muscles around those digits as he slowly, carefully began to twist and thrust them in and out of her, his thumb rubbing firmly over her clit in slow, deliberate circles until she was nearly out of her mind with pleasure.

His lips were at her throat again, kissing and sucking at her damp flesh aggressively, intent on marking her as his even as he continued to pleasure her to the brink of climax. When Miriel finally tipped over the edge, it felt as though the tremendous pressure that had been building within her groin had literally exploded. She violently shuddered as wave after wave of pleasure crashed through her body, inundating her senses so completely that she was unable to breathe for what felt like an eternity.

And still, Kirion continued to thrust his fingers into her, softly kissing her along her cheeks and lips until her arching hips collapsed back down to the ground. With one final lick and kiss to her mouth, Kirion removed his fingers and sat up to push his breeches down just far enough to free his engorged member.

He moved back to position himself at her entrance, rubbing the head of his cock teasingly along her crease and against her still-throbbing clit a few times before abruptly thrusting into her passage all the way to the hilt. Miriel cried out and arched up against his groin as a sharp jolt of pain shot up her spine, but then she wrapped her legs tightly around his waist and reached up with trembling arms to pull him down flush onto her body.

Kirion paused for a moment, his eyes closed and his forehead pressed against her own, allowing her to adjust to the considerable girth stretching her virgin passage. His fingers had loosened her somewhat, but she was still incredibly tight. Only when her trembling slowed and she began to squirm a little beneath him did he open his eyes and begin to thrust his hips in a slow, steady rhythm.

Miriel's fingers clutched at the robes covering his back as the king's deep, powerful thrusts rubbed against sensitive places inside of her that she never knew she had, stoking the flames of her pleasure once again. She could almost feel his eyes touching her as he watched her face intently without ever once losing his rhythm.

She struggled to hold his gaze, wanting to see the moment of his climax, to maybe see him lose a little of that powerful, kingly demeanor and know it was *she* that had made him lose it. As if reading her thoughts, Kirion smiled and lowered his head to kiss her breathless, his hips beginning to increase their speed until he had once again stroked her into climax. It wasn't until he gave one final, heavy thrust and a flood of warmth coated her passage that Miriel realized she had closed her eyes as she came, opening them in enough time to see Kirion's face contort for a few beats in ecstasy.

His face in passion was as beautiful as his smile.

CHAPTER 7

It was probably lucky that this had occurred within the human realm. Miriel imagined that they would have been half-frozen by now if Kirion had dared taken her while lying amongst the drifts that currently surrounded the Lithviri palace. As it were, the flurries of snow the wind blew across their partially exposed bodies as they lay intertwined on top of her cloak felt as gentle and pleasant as a cool breeze instead of painfully bone-chilling. She had often lamented her shadowy state while exploring the human realm, but after tonight, she would never complain again.

"Can you tell me," Kirion said, breaking the comfortable silence of the sated that had fallen between them, "how a human child ended up as the Lithviri princess?"

Miriel lifted her head from his chest to look up at

him. She had known this question would inevitably come and had prepared herself well for it.

"The king found me wandering around the Inbetween when I was five," she replied, "hungry, thirsty, and scared in a place that might as well have been on a different planet."

One blond eyebrow arched higher. "The Inbetween? How in the name of the High Powers were you able to enter without the help of a Sidhe?"

"I honestly do not know. Father believes that I stumbled upon an old doorway that had been forgotten. All I know is that one moment, I was running through the woods behind my house, and then between one blink and the next, I was suddenly running across a field of wildflowers beneath a gray sky."

Kirion absently stroked her hair. "Young as you were, were you unable to name your home?"

Miriel shook her head. "Had he taken me back into the human realm through a doorway of his own making, it would have been impossible to find my home again no matter how long we searched." She gestured to the decorations all around them. "It is the same reason why I knew the meaning behind all of this. This society, this era of human history is very close to the one where I was born."

His hand stilled. "A human child of the future…"

"Yes, though we did not discover this until Father began to take me into the human realm after a couple of decades of living within the elven realm, and I realized it was the human realm as it had been several thousand years in the past. Thus, there was no doorway besides the one that had initially brought me across time and space that could send me home, and it was never found. The Rift we crossed on this night to come here may very well be the same one, but it does not matter. The family I left behind was an abusive one, and I have no desire to reclaim my humanity."

"Then why come here at all?"

Miriel smiled sheepishly. "I suppose for sentimental reasons. The season of Christmas and all the spectacle that surrounds it was something I loved as a child. It was the one bright spot in so many dark memories."

Kirion shook his head. "I find it remarkable that Arandur and Isilya have managed to keep the secret of your human origins for so long."

"Only they and Elion know the truth. Father performed the transmutation on my body, himself."

"He *is* an exceptional mage," Kirion agreed. "I must be certain to thank him thoroughly for the extraordinary gift he has provided me."

Miriel wrinkled her nose in confusion. "Gift?"

He leaned down and kissed her softly on the nose. "My new bride."

"You—are that certain that you want me?" Miriel asked, suddenly feeling bashful.

"Did I not just prove to you that I was?" he said, his hand trailing down her back to squeeze her bottom playfully.

Rather than feel embarrassed, his actions brought a mischievous smile to her face. "I must warn you that my mother is quite content in having me unwed and living in the palace indefinitely."

Kirion smiled and hugged her more tightly against his chest. "Then perhaps it is fortunate that we have the whole of winter and spring to change her mind."

WHEN MIRIEL and Kirion finally reentered the ballroom an indeterminate amount of time later, her arm threaded casually in his, her face was so stiff with her efforts to give no hints to what had just transpired between her and the Supreme King that she wondered if it would soon start to ache. She studiously avoided looking anyone directly in the eye as Kirion led her towards the head table where her parents sat watching them approach with deceptively casual expressions, though her mother's eyes were locked on their intertwined arms.

The whispers from the courtiers that followed immediately in their wake were a thousand times harder to ignore. The gossipmongers at court were certainly getting plenty of fuel to ignite the flames of the rest of the night's speculations regarding their Supreme King's true purpose for visiting. No matter her parents' initial misgivings, a royal announcement about her betrothal to the Supreme King would come fairly soon, she was sure. She would not spoil their fun by giving the game away here.

"Ah, so you have found our wayward princess," her father said with a laugh as though his hands were not clenched with tension beneath the table.

"A rather fortuitous but welcomed meeting," Kirion replied with a genial smile as he led Miriel to her previous seat next to the queen before reclaiming his own at the head of the table. "We had the most delightful conversation while walking within the royal gardens."

It took every drop of discipline Miriel had within her to keep herself from blushing. "Conversation," indeed.

"I see," her father said, both his tone and the slight narrowing of his eyes speaking volumes.

However, instead of avoiding her parents' eyes as she

desperately wanted to, Miriel met her father's suspicious gaze calmly with a small smile. She could no longer be the shy Lithviri princess, not if she wished for the people of the Second Realm to accept her as their new Supreme Queen. However, she would need to convince her parents first of her resolve, that marrying Kirion was truly what she *wanted* and not what she thought was *expected* of her.

Feeling her mother's eyes on her, Miriel shifted her gaze from her stare-down with her father to find her mother watching her just as closely with an unreadable expression. Instead of suffering through what would likely be marks of tedious pleasantries without any real substance while both her parents tried to inconspicuously determine what had occurred between Kirion and her, perhaps a demonstration was in order.

"I think tonight, I am in a mood to dance," she announced suddenly into the tense silence that had fallen over the table.

Her mother's eyes instantly widened in a brief instant of habitual panic before regaining her serene expression just as quickly, likely remembering that the Supreme King had already touched her.

Kirion offered Miriel a slight nod, amusement flashing briefly in his eyes. "Then by all means, allow me to be your partner."

"I would be delighted, Your Majesty," Miriel accepted without hesitation, rising from her seat and taking his extended hand."

"Care to join us in the dance?" Kirion asked, offering his hosts what was likely his first smile in their presence. "It is, after all, a night of celebration."

After slowly glancing at both his daughter and the Supreme King in turn, Arandur's entire demeanor finally changed into something a bit more relaxed. "It is, indeed."

Miriel couldn't help squeezing Kirion's hand in growing excitement, for the dance and for the many things she would experience at Kirion's side in the future. With her father on their side, maybe it wouldn't take until spring to receive her mother's blessings, after all.

Elven King Series Book One

For Emily Ford, being awakened in the dead of night by what seems to be the very shadows in her bedroom come to life is the least of her worries as she is spirited away to become the new wife of an elven king for the purpose of bearing his heirs.

But can a human ever really win the heart of an elf or have a place within the elven court? Especially when the biggest obstacles to both are her new husband's barren and resentful queen, who has no qualms about wanting Emily gone and is prepared to do the unspeakable to make it happen, and the whispers of anti-human sentiments within the elven court, itself? **(Also includes the bonus short: *Date Night*.)**

NOW AVAILABLE

ABOUT THE AUTHOR

Cristina Rayne is a *New York Times* and *USA Today* best-selling author who lives in West Texas with her crazy cat and about a dozen bookcases full of fantasy worlds and steamy romances. She has a degree in Computer Science which totally qualifies her to write romances. As Fantasy is her first love, she feels if she can inject a little love into the fantastical, along with a few steamy scenes, then all the better. She is the author of the *Elven King, The Elven Realms, Riverford Shifters, Dragon Shifters of Elysia, Incarnations of Myth, The Vampire Underground* paranormal romance series, and the *Fractured Multiverse* science-fantasy series.

For More Information:
www.cristinarayneauthor.com